PINEAPPLE POET
and the
CURSE
of the
Smoothie Man

by Cam MacMillan
illustrations by Don Gauthier

Mutual Publishing

For
Davey, Mike, Peter and Mickey
John, Paul, George and Ringo
Mick, Keith, Ron, Charlie, and Brian,
Peter, Paul and Mary,
Cass, Michelle, John and Denny,
and
Lorraine and Max
(Who were never afraid of the Smoothie Man)

Text and character design copyright © 2002 by Cam MacMillan
Illustrations copyright © 2003 by Don Gauthier

Library of Congress Catalog Card
Number: 2003109952

ISBN 1-56647-642-9

Layout by Jane Hopkins

First Printing, November 2003
1 2 3 4 5 6 7 8 9

Mutual Publishing
1215 Center Street, Suite 210
Honolulu, Hawaii 96816
Ph: (808) 732-1709
Fax: (808) 734-4094
e-mail: mutual@mutualpublishing.com
www.mutualpublishing.com

Printed in Korea

I have a juicy
Story to share,
About when we were
Young and green.

open these leaves
If you dare,
They're not as scary
As they seem.

- Pineapple Poet

Pineapple Poet has a lot of fun.
No need to work when there's
    Plenty of sun.

Surfing all day at Big Wave Beach,
The waves too big
    For little guys to reach!

Then roasting all day
On the white hot sand,
He listens to K95
Playing his favorite band.

Pineapples have to stay tan,
You know.
It gives them that special
Green and gold glow.

7

Next catch something
For the supper dish,
Best place on the island for the
Humu Humu Fish!*

*Deep Blue Bay has a secret spot,
where fish bite anything that you got.

"**I**'ve been working too hard,
　　Gotta slow down,
Life's too short to rush around.

Another day like this,
　　I'll get stressed out.
Gotta pace myself,
　　Don't knock myself out!"

"**H**ave to take time to enjoy the day,
The easy going, carefree Pineapple way!"

"I'll start tomorrow," our Poet said.
"Oops! Time to put the little ones
Off to bed!"

13

"Time to sleep kids.
If you stay up late,

Smoothie Man will come
For the ones still awake.

14

With his shiny silver scoop
And his clear glass cup,

He'll measure exactly
How much to scoop up."

"He'll scoop you into cubes—
A perfect one inch square,

Toss out your skin,
Throw out your hair

And mix you in a drink
Called the 'Volcano Ka-Boom'

With all the other fruit
That have gone bad too soon."

"You're making it up!"
Said Pineapple Small.

"There's no scary guy
Thirty-six feet tall!

There's no knife, no cup,
No 'Volcano Ka-Boom'!

You just want us to stay
In our cozy little room!"

"**W**hen I was young like you,
Maybe a year or three older,

We had a crazy band called the
'**Fruit Bowl Soldiers**.'

We'd make fun
Of every little thing,

And stay up 'til
I could no longer sing."

"**W**alking home that night
Where I shouldn't have been,

Past the Spooky Hotel,
You know the one I mean?

I heard a noise
By the tall palm, see?
It sounded like chopping

But could it be? . . ."

"Smoothie Man!
Standing there in front of me!

Smoothie Man!
Bigger than the tallest tree!

Smoothie Man!
Saw me while I tried to scramble!

Smoothie Man!
Said,
'I need a cup of fresh Pineapple!'"

"He chased me over the Sharp Edged Rocks,

Up to the Forest of Cool Shady Walks,

26

Down the river called Icy Water Falling,

And into the Pool

of Hidden Spirits Calling."

27

"I thought I was safe
In the watery gloom.

Thought I had escaped
From my sudden doom

"But Smoothie Man is smart
He stayed very near—

Then he came after me...

With his
SCUBA GEAR!

"So I swam and I ran,
And I think as I run,

Smoothie Man isn't making
My life very fun.

If I wanted to ditch him
I'd need a good plan.

One that would work
On this dangerous man."

34

"One place on the Island
He couldn't go.
(At least, last I heard,
I don't think so!)

One place that Pineapples
Don't talk about.
I ran to that place called
'The Big Keep Out.'"

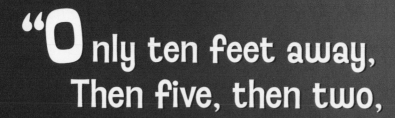

"**O**nly ten feet away,
Then five, then two,

And I jumped so high,
I
   lost
      my
         s h o e!

Over the fence,
Into the grass,

I laid down low
Waiting for
Smoothie Man to pass."

"Two million Pineapples
Slept in **The Big Keep Out**.

Nobody got in,
Without a doubt.

KEEP OUT!

With sixty miles of Electrified fence around

To guard all those Pineapples Snoring in the ground."

HAPPY HANK'S
PINEAPPLE PLANTATION
"WHERE
HAPPY
PINEAPPLES
GROW"

KEEP OUT!

"**H**ow I got out
Is another tale.
Nobody escapes from
The Big Keep Out jail.

So never go near
The Spooky Hotel I think,

Where Smoothie Man still makes
His Hawaiian Drink."

the end

Volcano Ka-Boom

1/2 cup water
1 cup ice
1 cup fresh pineapple
1 fresh mango
1/4 cup coconut milk
juice of 1/2 lime

Blend until smooth, then top
with a spurt of whipped cream.
Drizzle cherry shaved-ice syrup over
the cream for a 'lava' effect.

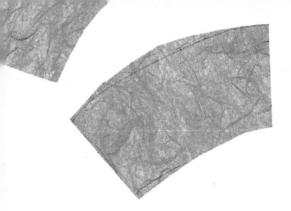

Icy Waterfall

Pineapple Poet's Favorite
(No Pineapple)

1/2 cup water
1 cup ice
1 cup watermelon (no seeds)
1 cup honeydew melon
juice of 1 lime

Blend until smooth!

Big Island

1 cup ice
1/2 cup ice cream or non-fat yogurt
1/4 cup coconut milk
1 banana, peeled
1 cup pineapple
1 cup honeydew melon

Pre-freeze some tall clear glasses. Blend the above ingredients until smooth. Pour mixture into a bowl, then store in freezer. Then, blend until smooth the following ingredients:

juice of 1 lime
1 cup watermelon
1 cup cantaloupe
1 mango
1/2 cup strawberries
1/2 cup peaches

Layer the two mixtures, parfait-style, in the frozen glasses. Add chocolate syrup, grenadine, or cherries and their juice between the layers if you want. Then insert a large spoon in the glasses, and twirl it upwards to swirl the contents.
Top with whipped cream.

Cam MacMillan

Cam makes sushi, coaches Little League, watches Ultra-Man on TV, and rides his bike a lot. In his spare time he designs 3D animations of molecular biological processes for doctors.

This is his first book about a surfing pineapple.

Don Gauthier

Don draws cartoons for fun and paints pictures for books and movies when people ask him to. He has three sons who grow at a scientifically impossible rate.

This is his first book about frightened fruit.

"Life's short but can be very sweet."

—Pineapple Poet